Bottoms Up!

Jeanne Willis

illustrated by Adam Stower

PUFFIN

Mummies and Daddies, why are we unhappy?

And when we are potty-trained, what do you do?

You make us put pants on and this we pooh-pooh.

Do piglets wear panties?
Or puppies or bears?
Do fox cubs wear boxers?
No, nobody cares!

Do kittens wear knickers?

Do bunnies wear bloomers?

Do **calves** put on **bras**
  to **disguise** their **bazoomers**?

Are tiger cubs made to run round in their trunks?

And what about squirrels?

And what about skunks?

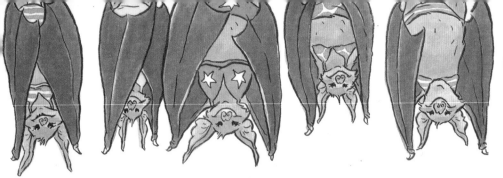

Do bats wear bikinis?

Do badgers wear briefs?

Do bullocks wear breeches to hide their beneaths?

Do lions wear loin cloths
to keep out the breeze?
Do donkeys wear droopy drawers
down to their knees?

Do wombats think,
"Ooh, I must cover
my willy"?

No, they do **not**,
because **that** would be **silly**.

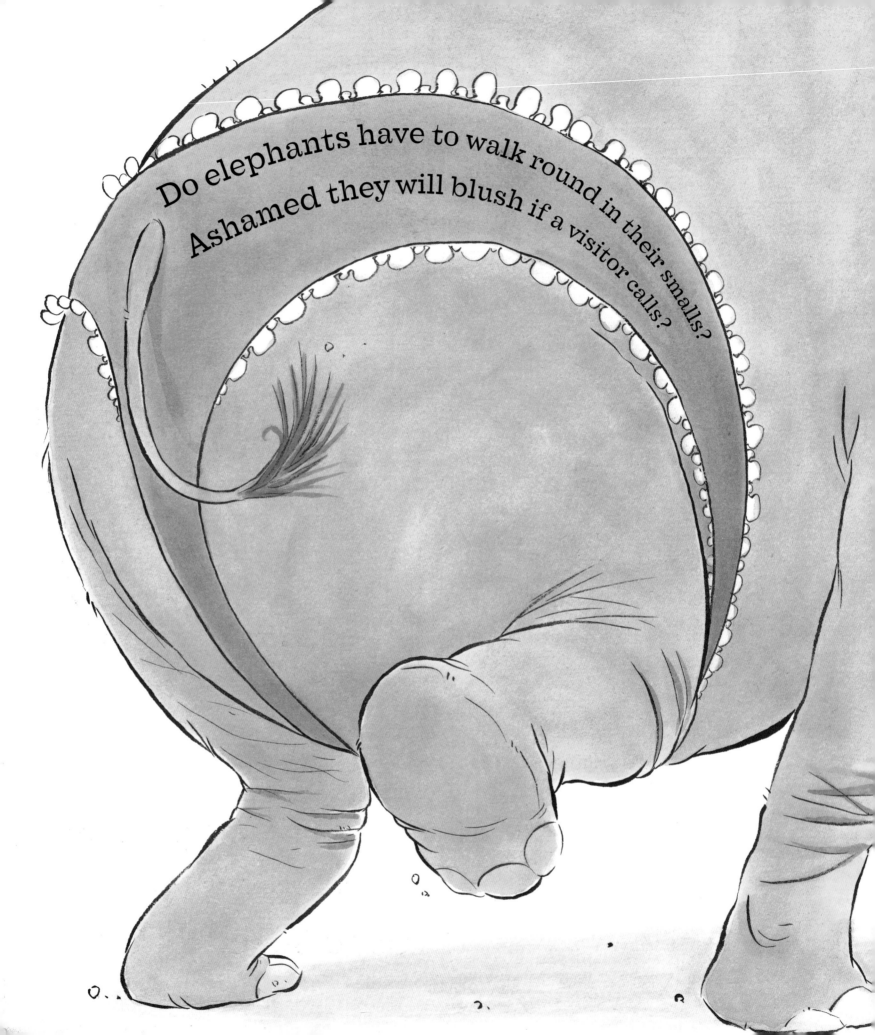

Do elephants have to walk round in their smalls?
Ashamed they will blush if a visitor calls?

No, they do **not**,
    because **nobody** minds.
So **why** can't the rest of us
    bare our behinds?

A bottom is truly a wonderful thing.

We can sit on it, shuffle and

shimmy
and swing.

So **why** must you wrap us
in paper and plastic,
and **tickle** our **tummies**
with **knicker elastic?**

Down with our pants!

Fling those nappies away!

Bottoms up,
babies and toddlers...

HOORAY!

For Ruth Dale, for being my friend
since we were barely out of nappies – J.W.

For Zoë and wombats everywhere – A.S. x

PUFFIN BOOKS
Published by the Penguin Group: London, New York, Australia,
Canada, India, Ireland, New Zealand and South Africa
Penguin Books Ltd, Registered Offices: 80 Strand, London WC2R 0RL, England

puffinbooks.com

First published 2009
1 3 5 7 9 10 8 6 4 2
Text copyright © Jeanne Willis, 2009
Illustrations copyright © Adam Stower, 2009
Made and printed in China
ISBN: 978-0-141-50213-7